Warrington & Vale Royal College
Learning Resource
KT-194-832
A110529

friends?

Dee Phillips

READZONE

READZONE BOOKS

First published in this edition 2016

ReadZone Books Limited
Visit our website: www.readzonebooks.com

All rights reserved. No part of this publication may be reproduced, stored in a retrieval system, or transmitted, in any form, or by any means, electronic, mechanical, photocopying, or otherwise, without the prior permission of ReadZone Books Limited.

© Copyright Ruby Tuesday Books Limited 2009

© Copyright in this edition ReadZone Books 2016

The right of the Author to be identified as the Author of this work has been asserted by the Author in accordance with the Copyright, Designs and Patents Act 1988.

Every attempt has been made by the Publisher to secure appropriate permissions for material reproduced in this book. If there has been any oversight we will be happy to rectify the situation in future editions or reprints. Written submissions should be made to the Publishers.

British Library Cataloguing in Publication Data (CIP) is available for this title.

ISBN 9781783222087

Printed in Malta by Melita Press

Developed and Created by Ruby Tuesday Books Ltd
Project Director – Ruth Owen
Consultant – Lorraine Petersen

Images courtesy of Shutterstock

ACKNOWLEDGEMENTS

With thanks to Lorraine Petersen, Chief Executive of NASEN, for her help in the development and creation of these books

That night I went online.
There was a message.
Join the group:
Sam Clark is so fat she killed her horse.

friends?

The room is very hot.
We are all waiting.
I look at Mum.
She says, "It will be OK, Gaby."

But I don't know.

I wish I could turn
back time.

It started one Saturday morning.
I was online with my friends.

Gaby:

What are we doing today?

Alisha:

I want to go into town.

Olly might be there.

Kelly:

Not Olly again!!!!!

Ella:

You are SO sad Alisha.

I add Sam to my friends list.

Sam was my friend ages ago.
Then her dad got rich.
Her family moved away.
Sam went to a private school.

Sam was in my class on Monday.
She looked sad.
She said, "Dad lost all our money.
We had to sell our house."

Sam said, "I really miss Bobbie."

Alisha said, "Is Bobbie your boyfriend?"

Sam said, "No. He's my horse. I had to sell him."

I saw Alisha give Ella a look.

I felt sorry for Sam.

That afternoon it was basketball.
I picked the team. Alisha. Kelly. Ella.
Alisha said, "Pick Carly. She's good."

But Sam was on her own.
I picked Sam.
Alisha said, "No way!"

We lost the game.

Alisha was angry.

Sam said, "Sorry. I'm rubbish at sports."

Alisha said, "You should stick to horses."

Then she walked off with Ella.

That night Alisha was still angry.

Alisha:
My Little Pony totally lost us the game.

Ella:
My Little Pony. LOL.

Gaby:
Just leave it A.

Alisha:
Whose side are you on Gaby?

I logged off.
Alisha would get bored with this.
She always did.

Sam wasn't at school on Tuesday.
Or Wednesday.

Alisha:

Where's My Little Pony?

Kelly:

Maybe she's gone back to her posh school.

On Thursday there was a message.

Sam:

I've been really upset.
Bobbie's new owner called me.
Bobbie broke his leg and
had to be shot.
RIP. Bobbie.

Sam came to school on Friday.
But she kept crying.

Alisha said, "God. It was only a horse."

Sam got really upset. She shouted, "You're so stupid. You don't know anything!"

Alisha was really angry.

Friday night we were online.

Alisha:

My Little Pony is SO stuck up.

Gaby:

Don't be mean Alisha.

Alisha:
She smells like a horse!

Kelly:
LOL

Ella:
You are SO bad Alisha.

Alisha:
MLP is so fat.
No wonder her horse's leg broke!

Saturday night was the same.

I logged off.
Alisha would get bored soon.
She always did.

Alisha:

Did you see MLP in McDonald's?

Kelly:

I thought I could smell a horse.

Alisha:

Maybe Bobbie is a burger now.

Ella:

Yuck! You are sick Alisha.

Sam:

Leave me alone.
What have I done to you?

Alisha:

MLP is a stuck up cow.

Kelly:

Boo hoo. Leave me alone.

Ella:

What have I done to you?

Boo hoo.

Alisha:

God I hate her.

On Monday Sam wasn't at school.

That night I went online.
There was a message.

Join the group:

Sam Clark is so fat
she killed her horse.

On Tuesday night I went online.
There was just one message.

Sam:

STOP. Please.

Then Mrs. Clark phoned Mum.

That's why we're here.
Mum and I.
Mr. and Mrs. Clark.

Mrs. Clark says, "Thanks for coming
Gaby. You are a good friend."

But I don't know.

Sam took lots of painkillers.
The doctors are trying to wake her up.

So now we are all just waiting.
Waiting in this hot room.

A doctor comes in.
I look down at my phone.
Mr. and Mrs. Clark stand up.

I look at the doctor's face.
I press send.

Gaby:

I'm sorry.
Your friend.

SAFER NETWORKING
ON YOUR OWN

Social networking sites can be great fun, but if they are abused they can cause a lot of unhappiness.

- Make up a name for a new networking site.
- List some special features of the new site. Try to think of things that no other sites have!
- Write a "behaviour code" for people using your site. What other things could be done to make networking safer?

WHAT WOULD YOU DO?
WITH A PARTNER

The story is about a girl being bullied online. However, Sam was sad even before she got to Gaby's school.

Join the group:

Sam Clark is so fat she killed her horse.

- Look back through the book. Think of as many different reasons as you can to explain why Sam took the pills.
- What would you have done if you had been one of the friends?

WHO'S TO BLAME?

Discuss with your group who is to blame for what happened:

- Alisha because she leads the bullying?
- Ella or Kelly, for encouraging Alisha?
- Gaby, for standing by and letting it happen?
- Sam, for letting the bullying get to her?
- Or perhaps the Internet is to blame?

HOW DOES IT END?

ON YOUR OWN / WITH A PARTNER / IN A GROUP

Does Sam live? Or does she die? Decide how the story ends and then imagine the next day.

- If you are working with a partner or in a group, role-play two or more of the characters meeting in town.

- If you are working on your own, create a computer screen that shows an online chat between the friends. How does each girl react to the news?

IF YOU ENJOYED
THIS BOOK,
TRY THESE OTHER
RiGHT NOW!
BOOKS.

Steve hates what he sees in
the mirror. Lizzie does, too.
Their lives would be so much
better if they looked different.

Mark's fighter jet is under
attack. There's only one way
to escape...

Lucy and Lloyd were in love,
but now it's over. So why is
Lloyd always watching her?

FIGHT

It's Saturday night.
Two angry guys. Two knives.
There's going to be a fight.

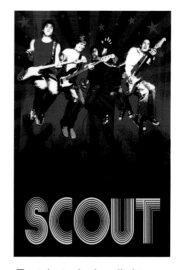

SCOUT

Tonight is the band's big
chance. Tonight, a record
company scout is at their gig!

BLAST

Ed's platoon is under attack.
Another soldier is in danger.
Ed must risk his own life to
save him.

DARE

It's just an old, empty house.
Lauren must spend the night
inside. Just Lauren and
the ghost...

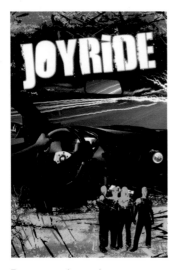

Dan sees the red car.
The keys are inside. Dan says
to Andy, Sam and Jess,
"Want to go for a drive?"

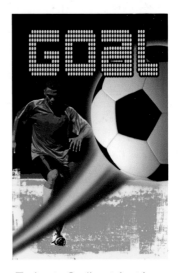

Today is Carl's trial with
City. There's just one place
up for grabs. But today,
everything is going wrong!

Sophie hates this new town.
She misses her friends.
There's nowhere to skate!

Tonight, Vicky must make a
choice. Stay in London with
her boyfriend Chris. Or start
a new life in Australia.